Today is F

Roger D. Aycock

Alpha Editions

This edition published in 2023

ISBN : 9789362099945

Design and Setting By
Alpha Editions
www.alphaedis.com
Email - info@alphaedis.com

As per information held with us this book is in Public Domain.
This book is a reproduction of an important historical work. Alpha
Editions uses the best technology to reproduce historical work in the same
manner it was first published to preserve its original nature. Any marks or
number seen are left intentionally to preserve its true form.

Contents

TODAY IS FOREVER..- 1 -

TODAY IS FOREVER

BY ROGER DEE

**Boyle knew there was an angle behind the aliens'
generosity ... but he had one of his own!**

"These Alcorians have been on Earth for only a month,"
David Locke said, "but already they're driving a wedge
between AL&O and the Social Body that can destroy the Weal
overnight. Boyle, it's got to be stopped!"

He put his elbows on Moira's antique conversation table and
leaned toward the older man, his eyes hot and anxious.

"There are only the two of them—Fermiirig and Santikh;
you've probably seen stills of them on the visinews a hundred
times—and AL&O has kept them so closely under cover that
we of the Social Body never get more than occasional rumors
about what they're really like. But I know from what I
overheard that they're carbonstructure oxygen-breathers with
a metabolism very much like our own. What affects them
physically will affect us also. And the offer they've made
Cornelison and Bissell and Dorand of Administrative Council
is genuine. It amounts to a lot more than simple longevity,
because the process can be repeated. In effect, it's—"

"*Immortality*," Boyle said, and forgot the younger man on the
instant.

The shock of it as a reality blossomed in his mind with a slow
explosion of triumph. It had come in his time, after all, and the
fact that the secret belonged to the first interstellar visitors to
reach Earth had no bearing whatever on his determination to
possess it. Neither had the knowledge that the Alcorians had
promised the process only to the highest of government

bodies, Administrative Council. The whole of AL&O—Administration, Legislation and Order—could not keep it from him.

"It isn't *right*," Locke said heatedly. "It doesn't fit in with what we've been taught to believe, Boyle. We're still a modified democracy, and the Social Body *is* the Weal. We can't permit Cornelison and Bissell and Dorand to take what amounts to immortality for themselves and deny it to the populace. That's tyranny!"

The charge brought Boyle out of his preoccupation with a start. For the moment, he had forgotten Locke's presence in Moira's apartment. He had even forgotten his earlier annoyance with Moira for allowing the sophomoric fool visitor's privilege when it was Boyle's week, to the exclusion of the other two husbands in Moira's marital-seven, to share the connubial right with her.

But the opportunity tumbled so forcibly into his lap was not one to be handled lightly. He held in check his contempt for Locke and his irritation with Moira until he had considered his windfall from every angle, and had marshalled its possibilities into a working outline of his coup to come.

He even checked his lapel watch against the time of Moira's return from the theater before he answered Locke. With characteristic cynicism, he took it for granted that Locke, in his indignation, had already shared his discovery with Moira, and in cold logic he marked her down with Locke for disposal once her purpose was served. Moira had been the most satisfactory of the four women in Boyle's marital-seven, but when he weighed her attractions against the possible immortality ahead, the comparison did not sway his resolution for an instant.

Moira, like Locke, would have to go.

"You're sure there was no error?" Boyle asked. "You couldn't have been mistaken?"

"I heard it," Locke said stubbornly.

He clenched his fists angrily, patently reliving his shock of discovery. "I was running a routine check on Administration visiphone channels—it's part of my work as communications technician at AL&O—when I ran across a circuit that had blown its scrambler. Ordinarily I'd have replaced the dead unit without listening to plain-talk longer than was necessary to identify the circuit. But by the time I had it tagged as a Council channel, I'd heard enough from Cornelison and Bissell and Dorand to convince me that I owed it to the Social Body to hear the rest. And now I'm holding a tiger by the tail, because I'm subject to truth-check. That's why I came to you with this, Boyle. Naturally, since you are President of Transplanet Enterprises—"

"I know," Boyle cut in, forestalling digression. Locke's job, not intrinsically important in itself, still demanded a high degree of integrity and left him open to serum-and-psycho check, as though he were an actual member of AL&O or a politician. "If anyone knew what you've overheard, you'd get a compulsory truth-check, admit your guilt publicly and take an imprisonment sentence from the Board of Order. But your duty came first, of course. Go on."

"They were discussing the Alcorians' offer of longevity when I cut into the circuit. Bissell and Dorand were all for accepting at once, but Cornelison pretended indecision and had to be coaxed. Oh, he came around quickly enough; the three of them are to meet Fermiirig and Santikh tomorrow morning at nine in the AL&O deliberations chamber for their injections. You should have heard them rationalizing that, Boyle. It would have sickened you."

"I know the routine—they're doing it for the good of the Social Body, of course. What puzzles me is why the Alcorians should give away a secret so valuable."

"Trojan horse tactics," Locke said flatly. "They claim to have arrived at a culture pretty much like our own, except for a superior technology and a custom of prolonging the lives of administrators they find best fitted to govern. They're posing as philanthropists by offering us the same opportunity, but actually they're sabotaging our political economy. They know that the Social Body won't stand for the Council accepting an immortality restricted to itself. That sort of discrimination would stir up a brawl that might shatter the Weal forever."

Deliberately, Boyle fanned the younger man's resentment. "Not a bad thing for those in power. But it *is* rough on simple members of the Social Body like ourselves, isn't it?"

"It's criminal conspiracy," Locke said hotly. "They should be truth-checked and given life-maximum detention. If we took this to the Board of Order—"

"No. Think a moment and you'll understand why."

Boyle had gauged his man, he saw, to a nicety. Locke was typical of this latest generation, packed to the ears with juvenile idealism and social consciousness, presenting a finished product of AL&O's golden-rule ideology that was no more difficult to predict than a textbook problem in elementary psychology. To a veteran strategist like Boyle, Locke was more than a handy asset; he was a tool shaped to respond to duty unquestioningly and to cupidity not at all, and therefore an agent more readily amenable than any mercenary could have been.

"But I *don't* understand," Locke said, puzzled. "Even Administration and Legislation are answerable to Order. It's the Board's duty to bring them to account if necessary."

"Administration couldn't possibly confirm itself in power from the beginning without the backing of Order and Legislation," Boyle pointed out. "Cornelison and Bissell and Dorand would have to extend the longevity privilege to the other two groups, don't you see, in order to protect themselves. And that means that Administrative Council is not alone in this thing—it's AL&O as a body. If you went to the Board of Order with your protest, the report would die on the spot. So, probably, would you."

He felt a touch of genuine amusement at Locke's slack stare of horror. The seed was planted; now to see how readily the fool would react to a logical alternative, and how useful in his reaction he might be.

"I know precisely how you feel," Boyle said. "It goes against our conditioned grain to find officials venal in this day of compulsory honesty. But it's nothing new; I've met with similar occasions in my own Transplanet business, Locke."

He might have added that those occasions had been of his own devising and that they had brought him close more than once to a punitive truth-check. The restraining threat of serum-and-psycho had kept him for the greater part of his adult life in the ranks of the merely rich, a potential industrial czar balked of financial empire by the necessity of maintaining a strictly legal status.

Locke shook himself like a man waking out of nightmare.

"I'm glad I brought this problem to a man of your experience," he said frankly. "I've got great confidence in your judgment, Boyle, something I've learned partly from watching you handle Transplanet Enterprises and partly from talking with Moira."

Boyle gave him a speculative look, feeling a return of his first acid curiosity about Locke and Moira. "I had no idea that Moira was so confidential outside her marital-seven," he said dryly. "She's not by any chance considering a *fourth* husband, is she?"

"Of course not. Moira's not *unconventional*. She's been kind to me a few times, yes, but that's only her way of making a practical check against the future. After all, she's aware it can't be more than a matter of—"

He broke off, too embarrassed by his unintentional blunder to see the fury that discolored the older man's face.

The iron discipline that permitted Boyle to bring that fury under control left him, even in his moment of outrage, with a sense of grim pride. He was still master of himself and of Transplanet Enterprises. Given fools enough like this to work with and time enough to use them, and he would be master of a great deal more. Immortality, for instance.

"She's quite right to be provident, of course," he said equably. "I *am* getting old. I'm past the sixty-mark, and it can't be more than another year or two before the rejuvenators refuse me further privilege and I'm dropped from the marital lists for good."

"Damn it, Boyle, I'm sorry," Locke said. "I didn't mean to offend you."

The potential awkwardness of the moment was relieved by a soft chime from the annunciator. The apartment entrance dilated, admitting Moira.

She came to them directly, slender and poised and supremely confident of her dark young beauty, her ermine wrap and high-coiled hair glistening with stray raindrops that took the light like diamonds. The two men stood up to greet her, and Boyle could not miss the subtle feminine response of her to Locke's eager, athletic youth.

If she's planning to fill my place in her marital-seven with this crewcut fool, Boyle thought with sudden malice, *then she's in for a rude shock. And a final one.*

"I couldn't enjoy a line of the play for thinking of you two patriots plotting here in my apartment," Moira said. "But then the performance was shatteringly dull, anyway."

Her boredom was less than convincing. When she had hung her wrap in a closet to be aerated and irradiated against its next wearing, she sat between Boyle and Locke with a little sigh of anticipation.

"Have you decided yet what to do about this dreadful immortality scheme of the Councils, darlings?"

Boyle went to the auto-dispenser in a corner and brought back three drinks, frosted and effervescing. They touched rims. Moira sipped at her glass quietly, waiting in tacit agreement with Locke for the older man's opinion.

"This longevity should be available to the Social Body as well as to AL&O," Boyle said. "It's obvious even to non-politicals like Locke and myself that, unless equal privilege is maintained, there's going to be the devil to pay and the Weal will suffer. It's equally obvious that the Alcorians' offer is made with the deliberate intent of undermining our system through dissension."

"To their own profit, of course," Locke put in. "Divide and conquer...."

"Whatever is to be done must be done quickly," Boyle said. "It would take months to negotiate a definitive plebiscite, and in that time the Alcorians would have gone home again without treating anyone outside AL&O. And there the matter would rest. It seems to be up to us to get hold of the longevity process ourselves and to broadcast it to the public."

"The good of the Body is the preservation of the Weal," Locke said sententiously. "What do you think, Moira?"

Moira touched her lips with a delicate pink tongue-tip, considering. To Boyle, her process of thought was as open as a plain-talk teletape; immortality for the Social Body automatically meant immortality for Moira and for David Locke. Both young, with an indefinite guarantee of life....

"Yes," Moira said definitely. "If some have it, then all should. But how, Philip?"

"You're both too young to remember this, of course," Boyle said, "but until the 1980 Truth-check Act, there was a whole field of determinative action applicable to cases like this. It's a simple enough problem if we plan and execute it properly."

His confidence was not feigned; he had gone over the possibilities already with the swift ruthlessness that had made him head of Transplanet Enterprises, and the prospect of direct action excited rather than dismayed him. Until now he had skirted the edges of illegality with painstaking care, never stepping quite over the line beyond which he would be liable to the disastrous truth-check, but at this moment he felt himself invincible, above retaliation.

"This present culture is a pragmatic compromise with necessity," Boyle said. "It survives because it answers natural problems that couldn't be solved under the old systems. Nationalism died out, for example, when we set up a universal government, because everyone belonged to the same Social Body and had the same Weal to consider. Once we realized that the good of the Body is more important than personal privacy, the truth-check made ordinary crime and political machination obsolete. Racial antagonisms vanished under deliberate amalgamation. Monogamy gave way to the marital-seven, settling the problems of ego clash, incompatability, promiscuity and vice that existed before. It also settled the disproportion between the male and female population.

"But stability is vulnerable. Since it never changes, it cannot stand against an attack either too new or too old for its immediate experience. So if we're going after this Alcorian longevity process, I'd suggest that we choose a method so long out of date that there's no longer a defense against it. *We'll take it by force!*"

It amused him to see Moira and Locke accept his specious logic without reservation. Their directness was all but childlike. The thought of engaging personally in the sort of cloak-and-sword adventure carried over by the old twentieth-century melodrama tapes was, as he had surmised, irresistible to them.

"I can see how you came to be head of Transplanet, Boyle," Locke said enviously. "What's your plan, exactly?"

"I've a cottage in the mountains that will serve as a base of operations," Boyle explained. "Moira can wait there for us in the morning while you and I take a 'copter to AL&O. According to your information, Cornelison and Bissell and Dorand will meet the Alcorians in the deliberations chamber at nine o'clock. We'll sleep-gas the lot of them, take the longevity process and go. There's no formal guard at Administration, or anywhere else, nowadays. There'll be no possible way of tracing us."

"Unless we're truth-checked," Locke said doubtfully. "If any one of us should be pulled in for serum-and-psycho, the whole affair will come out. The Board of Order—"

"Order won't know whom to suspect," Boyle said patiently. "And they can't possibly check the whole city. They'd have no way of knowing even that it was someone from this locale. It could be anyone, from anywhere."

When Locke had gone and Moira had exhausted her fund of excited small talk, Boyle went over the entire plan again from inception to conclusion. Lying awake in the darkness with only the sound of Moira's even breathing breaking the stillness, he let his practical fancy run ahead.

Years, decades, generations—what were they? To be by relative standards undying in a world of ephemerae, with literally nothing that he might not have or do....

He dreamed a dream as old as man, of stretching today into forever.

Immortality.

The coup next morning was no more difficult, though bloodier, than Boyle had anticipated.

At nine sharp, he left David Locke at the controls of his helicar on the sun-bright roof landing of AL&O, took a self-service elevator down four floors and walked calmly to the deliberation chamber where Administrative Council met with the visitors from Alcor. He was armed for any eventuality with an electronic freeze-gun, a sleep-capsule of anesthetic gas, and a nut-sized incendiary bomb capable of setting afire an ordinary building.

His first hope of surprising the Council in conference was dashed in the antechamber, rendering his sleep-bomb useless. Dorand was a moment late; he came in almost on Boyle's heels, his face blank with astonishment at finding an intruder ahead of him.

The freeze-gun gave him no time for questions.

"Quiet," Boyle ordered, and drove the startled Councilor ahead of him into the deliberations chamber.

He was just in time. Cornelison had one bony arm already bared for the longevity injection; Bissell sat in tense anticipation of his elder's reaction; the Alcorian, Fermiirig, stood at Cornelison's side with a glittering hypodermic needle in one of his four three-fingered hands.

For the moment, a sudden chill of apprehension touched Boyle. There should have been *two* Alcorians.

"Quiet," Boyle said again, this time to the group. "You, Fermiirig, where is your mate?"

The Alcorian replaced the hypodermic needle carefully in its case, his triangular face totally free of any identifiable emotion and clasped both primary and secondary sets of hands together as an Earthman might have raised them overhead. His eyes, doe-soft and gentle, considered Boyle thoughtfully.

"Santikh is busy with other matters," Fermiirig said. His voice was thin and reedy, precise of enunciation, but hissing faintly on the aspirants. "I am to join her later—" his gentle eyes went to the Councilors, gauging the gravity of the situation from their tensity, and returned to Boyle—"if I am permitted."

"Good," Boyle said.

He snapped the serum case shut and tucked it under his arm, turning toward the open balcony windows. "You're coming with me, Fermiirig. You others stay as you are."

The soft drone of a helicar descending outside told him that Locke had timed his descent accurately. Cornelison chose that moment to protest, his wrinkled face tight with consternation at what he read of Boyle's intention.

"We know you, Boyle! You can't possibly escape. The Ordermen—"

Boyle laughed at him.

"There'll be no culprit for the Ordermen," he said, "nor any witnesses. You've wiped out ordinary crime with your truth-checks and practicalities, Cornelison, but you've made the way easier for a man who knows what he wants."

He pressed the firing stud of his weapon. Cornelison fell and lay stiffly on the pastel tile. Bissell and Dorand went down as quickly, frozen to temporary rigidity.

Boyle tossed his incendiary into the huddle of still bodies and shoved the Alcorian forcibly through the windows into the hovering aircar.

Locke greeted the alien's appearance with stark amazement. "My God, Boyle, are you *mad*? You can't kidnap—"

The dull shock of explosion inside the deliberations chamber jarred the helicar, throwing the slighter Alcorian to the floor and staggering Boyle briefly.

"Get us out of here," Boyle said sharply. He turned the freeze-gun on the astounded Locke, half expecting resistance and fully prepared to meet it. "You fool, do you think I'm still playing the childish game I made up to keep you and Moira quiet?"

A pall of greasy black smoke poured after them when Locke, still stunned by the suddenness of catastrophe, put the aircar into motion and streaked away across the city.

Boyle, watching the first red tongue of flame lick out from the building behind, patted the serum case and set himself for the next step.

Immortality.

Locke took the helicar down through the mountains, skirting a clear swift river that broke into tumultuous falls a hundred yards below Boyle's cottage, and set it down in a flagstone court.

"Out," Boyle ordered.

Moira met them in the spacious living room, her pretty face comical with surprise and dismay.

"Philip, what's *happened?* You look so—"

She saw the alien then and put a hand to her mouth.

"Keep her quiet while I deal with Fermiirig," Boyle said to Locke. "I have no time for argument. If either of you gives me any trouble...."

He left the threat to Locke's stunned fancy and turned on the Alcorian.

"Let me have the injection you had ready for Cornelison. Now."

The Alcorian moved his narrow shoulders in what might have been a shrug. "You are making a mistake. You are not fitted for life beyond the normal span."

"I didn't bring you here to moralize," Boyle said. "If you mean to see your mate again, Fermiirig, give me the injection!"

"There was a time in your history when force was justifiable," Fermiirig said. "But that time is gone. You are determined?" He shook his head soberly when Boyle did not answer. "I was afraid so."

He took the hypodermic needle out of its case, squeezed out a pale drop of liquid and slid the point into the exposed vein of Boyle's forearm.

Boyle, watching the slow depression of the plunger, asked: "How long a period will this guarantee, in Earth time?"

"Seven hundred years," Fermiirig said. He withdrew the instrument and replaced it in its case, his liquid glance following Boyle's rising gesture with the freeze-gun. "At the end of that time, the treatment may be renewed if facilities are available."

Immortality!

"Then I won't need you any more," Boyle said, and rayed him down. "Nor these other two."

Locke, characteristically, sprang up and tried to shield Moira with his own body. "Boyle, what are you thinking of? You can't murder us without—"

"There's a very effective rapids a hundred yards down river," Boyle said. "You'll both be quite satisfactorily dead after going through it, I think. Possibly unrecognizable, too, though that doesn't matter particularly."

He was pressing the firing stud, slowly because something in the tension of the moment appealed to the sadism in his nature, when an Orderman's freeze-beam caught him from behind and dropped him stiffly beside Fermiirig.

The details of his failure reached him later in his cell, anticlimactically, through a fat and pimply jailer inflated to bursting with the importance of guarding the first murderer in his generation.

"AL&O kept this quiet until the Council killing," the turnkey said, "but it had to come out when the Board of Order went after you. The Alcorians are telepathic. Santikh led the Ordermen to your place in the mountains. Fermiirig guided her."

He grinned vacuously at his prisoner, visibly pleased to impart information. "Lucky for you we don't have capital punishment any more. As it is, you'll get maximum, but they can't give you more than life."

Lucky? The realization of what lay ahead of him stunned Boyle with a slow and dreadful certainty.

A sentence of life.

Seven hundred years.

Not immortality—

Eternity.

Milton Keynes UK
Ingram Content Group UK Ltd.
UKHW050925170424
441314UK00004B/220

9 789362 099945